My Reserve
of Thoughts

By- Gourav Ku. Sarangi (GKS)

Acknowledgement

This book is my first solo publication under the guidance of my beloved parents and family members. I am always blessed to have such a beautiful environment surrounding me in which I get inspired to work on my passion and continue my writing skills in literature.

I would also like to thanks my friends and relatives who kept on reading and reviewing my works and appreciated throughout the journey.

At last but not the least a special thanks to my father Shri Master Apollo and my mother Mrs. Sanjukta Dash for giving so much of love and care in upbringing my skills; side by side another thanks to my best buddy Miss Simran Rout who not only is a good friend but also has a lot of potential to be a good support.

Love you all!

THANK YOU!

<u>Forward</u>

Read my unique and self-made quotes belonging to various genres of love, heartbreak, motivation, etc.

Hope you guys love and enjoy reading it!

Keep on inspiring and getting inspired.

-:Quotes:-

Hope for the best, you will get better;

Hope for better you will get good;

Do something good you will always have a best result
with better compliments.

-GKS

Gone through many adventures,

Seen many curvatures,

Still left behind some better relives,

Gathering thoughts with simple vibes.

-GKS

You yourself is the protector and perisher
of your degree.

-GKS

Remembering the past emotions,

And hunting for better options,

Are almost the same working principles with different aspects.

-GKS

Going up to the pillar,

Leaving everything behind the base,

Goes on my dreams,

Breaking the contours of lace.

-GKS

There is a simple and single word from which peace arises "Love".

-GKS

Life of miscellaneous, and a lot of condolences, with bit of appreciation and initiation… Pardon me! Narrates the best futuristic idea.

-GKS

The one who shows off just because to have you as their part of life, will always sign for you; but the only one who really loves you and wants to make you his life will never call a word on you.

That's the sign of true love!

-GKS

Sometimes its really hard to get control over own mind as it doesn't work according to your hearty wishes neither your heart.

-GKS

When there is no value for your value,
You should stop valuing the valuation.

-GKS

When someone understands your feelings he/she becomes your reasoning; but someone turns your feelings to joke he/she becomes your probability.

-GKS

When you are up to live your standards, but get down to live with someone who has become your habit… Trust me! You are in true love.

-GKS

I hardly care for those who are just part of my life; but badly care for the one who is my life.

-GKS

My ego and attitude races till their extent but finishes at your existence.

-GKS

Some relations are meant to be celebrated wholely, because after a series durations of dissension also they won't splinter.

-GKS

No there is not any other options for the one's feelings for someone, neither maturity nor understanding matters.

-GKS

We change, we merge, We get our life in urge,
Finally, we make ourselves, An outstanding forge.

-GKS

Here we go through many hurdles,

Life restarts at every step with full throttles,

Caging our memories in taut bottles,

Brings us a drastic change in bundles,

Happy with the moment we move on giving self cuddles.

-GKS

Love,

In the eyes of a girl,

In the words of a boy,

The more rude they get,

The more possessive and truthful they are.

-GKS

Tragedy strikes back,

When the breakthrough of heart,

Starving for love,

Searches in the puddle,

Amity for juvenile soul.

-GKS

Perfect is the society, perfect is you

The one who is not perfect,

Is the coward mentality,

And the lagging soul of you.

-GKS

Why should we always try to have a sympathy regarding
undesired mood waves.

-GKS

Don't believe in sharing love, be the lover of yourself and find out who else loves you.

-GKS

Don't say me when you are done,
Tell me when you are up to do.

-GKS

We could not be resistance, but we should resist to all negativity.

-GKS

Do whatever you want, if there is no one who cares, why to care for them.

-GKS

Having someone who cheers you in success and tears your failures is like a sun which shines after dark and spring which brings the beauty back.

-GKS

Half of the time we try to speak with our destiny and the rest is destiny.

-GKS

Know your significance at your own methods of living in compatibility.

-GKS

The revolution happens in yourself when you decide to be revolutionary regarding your judgements.

-GKS

Yes we can do for our term, but we cannot take someone's part.

-GKS

Having a second choice is good but no second choice can replace the first one.

-GKS

Carry all your targeted efforts to a fixed success so that no delay will be a barrier to it.

-GKS

Get into the knowledge of replicating ideas into multiple work models.

-GKS

We though not change the way, but we should begin in
another.

-GKS

Call of destiny is never settled by any action that we do
right or wrong, it is to happen.

-GKS

High enough to the memories of beliefs, we remain in the
pathway to encourage our motivation.

-GKS

Cause for benefit is left behind the uncertainty of
transparency.

-GKS

Sometimes caring too much is toxic, but it is though natural.

-GKS

Red is not just a colour, we blush to it when feel for someone and wipe it out when hate someone.

-GKS

Not always we show the care, sometimes we bother a lot inside us.

-GKS

Self concession is important, to become yourself a package in you.

-GKS

Let's happen to begin in the new past and old present, where we learn more and execute wisely.

-GKS

Never be too compatible to any situation where you can't begin to step back.

-GKS

Some of us begin to create enough of space for us in our livelihood, but it's enough to make you create your own shell within you.

-GKS

Say hello to the sections of happiness which makes us believe the contradictory truth of self love.

-GKS

The letter that comprises emotion and comprises efforts, that letter I fill all my captions.

-GKS

Challenge yourself to the worst methodology and see what outcomes are awaiting.

-GKS

Don't meet your random destiny, make your destiny choose you from random choices.

-GKS

Don't move on because you had a past move on to do better than the past.

-GKS

We begin to learn from our past, but sometimes the same past begins deforming our worth yet learning.

-GKS

All of us must be strained in the after effects of time's unexpected reality.

-GKS

Most of the connections are tripped.
But some are tricky.

-GKS

We never chose to be inseparable soul, just we began to be in touch to never get separated.

-GKS

We break, we calm, we stand and move along;
Nothing remains same, only you and yours remains a long.

-GKS

We all are caught up in a tragic moment of unsung time.

-GKS

Once people step back from you, they never realise what's your worth to make them shine in you.

-GKS

Most of us think we have covered all the measures of life but life is experience not for expertise.

-GKS

All of a sudden we all have moved on from an era of fun
to era of facts.

-GKS

Jobs decide the experimental factor within you, but your
factor decide the worth of job for you.

-GKS

Sometimes we bother not about what we are going
through, but for the sake of not losing what we still have.

-GKS

Upgrade your ambitions to uplift your dead emotions,
because no heartless had a wholesome past.

-GKS

Sometimes we break and never get settled again, that's what we call as an end.

-GKS

Go beyond your limits, but never forget your limitations;
Be original and content yourself.

-GKS

Want less then expect more,
You'll surely fail in your expectations.

-GKS

Struggle till the efforts of getting the attachment back to your relation.

-GKS

Handle your sentiments till the meet
to the right sight.

-GKS

Lift up your thoughts to the limits where you stand by
them for fulfilment.

-GKS

The emotions are captured with contactless motion that
detects your soul of peace.

-GKS

Real are the beginning which begin to create charm
among hearts.

-GKS

To do is something to make it realise the real set.

-GKS

You are originally the person who had already made the thing move on, just you need to identify the time in topic.

-GKS

Next to the life there is a chance to win or lose a moment you have aim for.

-GKS

Roll down to compose a strategy in calming your wrath.

-GKS

Never lie to your present, let it know how dense your past went.

-GKS

Height of hardness is, two people feeling for each other but staying apart for ego.

-GKS

Realizing the fact that you have undergone a change from childhood to maturity is the most unrealistic approach.

-GKS

If we could teach on the matter we would have already done.

-GKS

Excuses are not which we make to hide lies, excuses are made to hide our journey for the upcoming success.

-GKS

Some quotes relax your brain and some stress the factor, choose wisely which you want to get as a supervisor.

-GKS

****

-THE END-